Date Due

FORM 109

SAVING THE NATURAL WORLD

UNDERSTANDING GLOBAL ISSUES

Published by Weigl Publishers Inc.
350 5th Avenue, Suite 3304, PMB 6G
New York, NY 10118-0069
Website: www.weigl.com

This book is based on *Saving the Natural World: Who cares about biodiversity?*
Copyright ©1997 Understanding Global Issues Ltd., Cheltenham, England

Library of Congress Cataloging-in-Publication Data
Redlin, Janice L. (ed.)
Saving the natural world / Janice L. Redlin, editor.
   p. cm. -- (Understanding global issues)
Includes bibliographical references and index.
ISBN 1-59036-236-5 (lib. bdg. : alk. paper) 1-59036-510-0 (ppk.)
1. Biological diversity conservation. 2. Nature--Effect of human beings on. 3.
Conservation of natural resources. I. Title. II. Series.
QH75.R433 2005
333.95'16--dc22

                    2004007075
       Printed in the United States of America
          1 2 3 4 5 6 7 8 9 0   10 09 08 07 06

EDITOR Janice L. Redlin **DESIGNER** Terry Paulhus

Contents

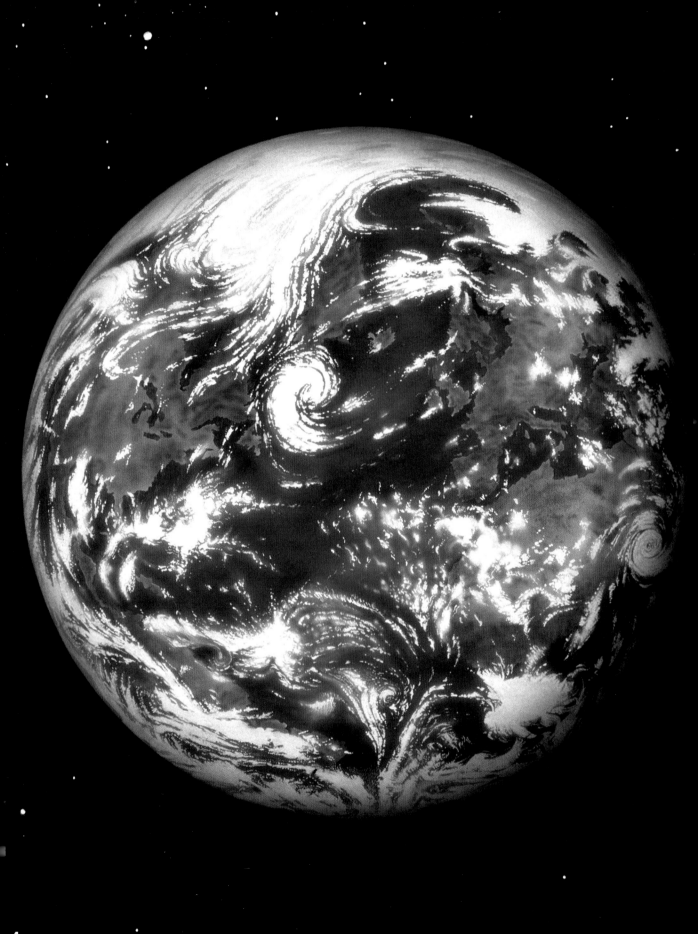

Introduction

Biodiversity is the very foundation of life on Earth, yet it is still very poorly understood. Earth was once as barren as Mars. Today, the delicately balanced **biosphere** in which we live depends on the complex interactions of many billions of organisms, plants, and animals. The healthy functioning of this life support system involves tiny creatures that break down organic matter in the soil; fungi that enable plant roots to absorb nutrients; marine **plankton** that transform sunlight into food energy; plants and trees that pump water from the ground to the atmosphere, thus producing rain; birds that carry seeds or eat insects; and so on. From ants to elephants, all have a part to play.

Meanwhile, **infrastructure** development on a giant scale is transforming Asia and Latin America. New roads, power plants, and water management systems are carving great strips through the natural landscapes of China, India, Mexico, Brazil, Indonesia, and Malaysia—countries that harbor some of the world's richest biodiversity. These countries also have high cultural diversity, with **indigenous** peoples who have survived close to nature for hundreds of years. These people are caught up in the tide of modernization. Their knowledge of local animals and plants is being gradually discarded.

The process of development is surely inevitable, irreversible and, for the poorest 80 percent of the world at least, a matter of basic human rights.

The scale of habitat destruction, **species** loss, pollution, and other disruption to the natural environment is already so great that it quite possibly places in jeopardy the entire life support system of the

> **Biodiversity is the very foundation of life on Earth, yet it is still very poorly understood.**

planet. Species loss today is estimated at 10,000 times the rate experienced before the **Industrial Revolution**. As many as half of all current species may be lost in the next 100 years. Meanwhile, species gain is taking place, too, as flora and fauna adapt to new conditions in a period of rapid environmental change. In addition to natural replacements, there will increasingly be artificial replacement and changes of those species most important for human society. All this poses new practical and ethical questions.

Conservationists point out the value of many plants and animals, including the aesthetic and spiritual nourishment that nature provides to man. For the world at large to benefit from, say, the medicinal value of a rare native plant, it must be synthesized, or intensively cultivated: nature alone cannot do it. Deciding which plants and animals to "domesticate" and which to keep in the wild raises difficult dilemmas.

Many people care about biodiversity. The question is: How much should be conserved? These problems cross continents and defy national frontiers. To have some hope of reaching effective solutions, a generally acceptable method must be found of assessing the risks, costs, and benefits—material, cultural, and spiritual—for all the millions of people affected by development and environmental change. The issues are hotly contested, and agreed solutions hard to find.

■■■ Earth is the only place where life is known to exist.

People's Place in Nature

It is easy for the urban citizen to imagine that the laws of nature somehow do not apply to human beings. While our ancestors lived in close proximity to animals and plants—sharing their hardship—urbanized humanity has distanced itself from the wild. Food is taken from supermarket shelves, its connection with living creatures and plants hardly acknowledged any more. Trees, plants, and animals have become part of the recreational landscape that we view through the window of a car or a television screen. We indulge our pets while handing over millions of domesticated "food animals" to factory production lines—out of sight, out of mind. Since the Industrial Revolution, we have created vast amounts of toxic waste that we have poured into the sea, river, soil, and air, damaging the very foundations upon which all life is built.

In short, we have lost track of the connection between human survival and the healthy operation of the natural world, in which clean air, fertile soil, and fresh water depend on "nature's web"—the millions of interdependent organisms that

■■■ **As more people gravitate toward city living, understanding of the human connection to nature is becoming lost.**

gradually transformed the barren world of four billion years ago into the living green planet we have inherited. Technology's latest brainchild, bioengineering, has reinforced the impression that we can control nature. Yet we breathe, eat, excrete, and die like every other living thing. We cannot escape our natural condition.

The biosphere within which life exists on Earth is a fragile and narrow band—as delicate as the fuzz on a peach. The conditions that make life possible for man are determined to a large degree by other living things—the forests that act as the lungs of the world, the organisms that make the soil fertile, the plants and plankton that begin the food chains on land and sea. Various parts of the planet's **ecosystems**—oceans,

---

Our own chances of survival will be enhanced if we work with, rather than against, nature.

---

soil, **ozone** layer—show visible signs of stress. If they break down altogether, human life itself could be threatened.

Nature is strong and healthy in the sense that it can recover quickly from the ravages of fire, disease, and other disasters. There is sometimes a vacuum left behind, though, and what fills it is often different from what went before. Nature undergoes continuous change, with **evolution** an unforgiving, relentless force. In that sense, the continuity of nature is a romantic illusion and its gentle harmony a myth. A closer look at that idyllic scene is likely to reveal a savage battleground, where the strong prey upon the weak and only the fittest survive. Humans are presently the dominant species—as the dinosaurs once were. Dinosaurs could do nothing to prevent their own extinction.

NATURAL SELECTION AND THE SURVIVAL OF THE FITTEST

The theory of natural selection, whereby individual organisms that are best adapted to their environment are more likely to survive and reproduce, originated in the 19th century with the biologist Charles Darwin.

Within individual species are great biological variations. These variations can include color, size, and physical abilities. How these variations interact with the environment determines the fitness of an individual or group within the species. Those with traits that allow for the strongest adaptive abilities stand the best chance of surviving, attracting mates, and reproducing.

The theory puts forward the idea that, through reproduction, environmental adaptations become hereditary, with the fittest of the species passing their adaptive traits to future generations. As part of the natural process, those individuals with weaker adaptive traits are eventually culled from the species.

PRESSURES ON BIODIVERSITY

One of the greatest threats to biodiversity is habitat loss due to human destruction. As the global population continues to increase, there is a need to continually develop land for residential communities, industries, and agriculture. Land development results in the removal of plant species from an area, creating a limited food supply for herbivorous animals, and eventually carnivores. Vegetation loss also results in soil erosion.

Human action has placed pressure on biodiversity in many other ways as well.

Hunting and Fishing

On many occasions, humans have overhunted various animal species so that they are not given the time to renew their numbers. Many have become extinct as a result. Numerous other species are endangered and are at great risk of being lost forever.

Energy

The extraction of non-renewable resources, such as crude oil, natural gas, oil sands, and coal, from the land to provide energy products causes the environment to be permanently altered. This has a negative impact on the plants and animals that depend on the area for their survival. Plants are often destroyed in pursuit of the resources. As a result, animals are often forced out of the area.

Pollution

Humans have polluted air, land, and bodies of water with waste and toxic chemicals. This pollution has created deformities and abnormalities in many species, and in others, has caused death.

Forestry

Human need for wood and wood products is resulting in the loss of the world's trees. Forests are home to many unique species of plants and animals, many of which rely on the forest habitat for survival. The loss of habitat often leads to the loss of these animals and plants. Forestry also plays a role in climate change, specifically global warming. Trees absorb carbon dioxide, a greenhouse gas that helps keep Earth warm. However, with fewer trees, less carbon dioxide is absorbed, making Earth warmer than it should be and causing harm to the environment and all living things in it.

Invasive Species

Human mobility has introduced new species of plants and animals into areas where they otherwise would not live. These plants and animals alter the ecological relationships that exist within the ecosystems when they compete with others for habitat and food.

NATURE'S WEB

The interdependent relationships of animals and plants within an ecosystem are complex and operate on several levels, most often described as an energy pyramid. Most ecosystems use sunlight as their original energy source. Plants use this energy to create food. For this reason, plants are also known as producers. Herbivores, otherwise known as primary consumers, feed on the producers, thus providing the herbivores with energy. Carnivores sit at the top of the energy pyramid, both as secondary and tertiary consumers. Secondary consumers receive their energy by feeding on primary consumers, while tertiary consumers feed on both primary and secondary consumers. Decomposers are found at various levels as they feed on organic matter, including the remains of the animals and plants. Energy is lost as it is moves up the levels of the pyramid. Therefore, there are fewer animals at the top of the pyramid than at the bottom.

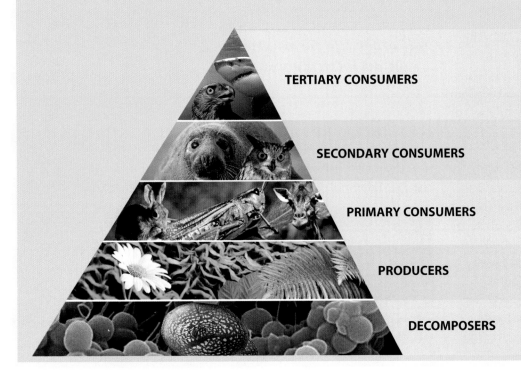

TERTIARY CONSUMERS

SECONDARY CONSUMERS

PRIMARY CONSUMERS

PRODUCERS

DECOMPOSERS

KEY CONCEPTS

Biodiversity Biodiversity refers to the variety of plant, animal, fungus, and microbial species found on Earth and the various ecosystems, or habitats, in which they live. Evolving over time, organisms have become uniquely adapted to particular ecosystems, and the removal or extinction of any one species can have far-reaching and often destructive effects. If an ecosystem's delicate balance is upset, air quality, soil quality, and even rainfall can be affected. As habitats are destroyed, hundreds of thousands of species—and potential medical cures and nutrient-rich foods—are forever lost.

Bioengineering Bioengineering brings together physical, chemical, or mathematical sciences and engineering methods and techniques for the study of biology, medicine, behavior, or health.

Does Biodiversity Matter?

The thought of a world without tigers, elephants, and whales is depressing, but their loss would not make life impossible for humans. The disappearance of other less famous creatures—soil-dwelling worms or fungi, for example, could be much more devastating for the future of mankind. The gradual degradation of soil, water, and air is hard to measure and combat, yet is potentially far more dangerous than the loss of lions or rhinos.

The total number of species on the planet is impossible to gauge accurately. Relatively few species have been studied in detail, and there is still only a basic understanding of how the different species interact with each other in the biosphere. Mammals, birds, fish, bacteria, plants, trees, and all other life forms work in an intricate web. They maintain the physical conditions—breathable air, the fresh water cycle, the supply of nutrients—that make Earth habitable.

Biodiversity also provides a massive resource of food, medicines, and other commercial products. More and more cropland is being planted with high-yielding, but genetically

uniform, varieties. Most food is provided by 15 to 20 plant species, such as rice, maize and wheat. Yet, as more production is concentrated into fewer high-

---

Mammals, birds, fish, bacteria, plants, trees, and all other life forms work in an intricate web.

---

yielding species, genetic erosion occurs, making the world's basic food supply vulnerable to new diseases, pests, or climate change. Keeping a large pool of

wild varieties of food plants is an essential insurance policy.

Most people in **developing countries** rely on traditional medicines—extracts of plants and animals. These medicines have varying degrees of effectiveness, and local doctors often prefer modern drugs. The World Health Organization (WHO) estimates that anywhere from 35,000 to 70,000 plants and herbs have been used for medicinal purposes. While the use of synthetic drugs is increasing, many natural extracts cannot be reproduced artificially or are less effective.

■ Ginseng is a popular herb. It is believed to increase blood supply and improve circulation.

Even so, concludes the World Conservation Monitoring Centre (WCMC), the vast majority of plant and animal species probably have little potential for being directly useful to humans. In terms of their direct economic value, most species could in theory be tossed. Just how many species can be killed off without sparking an ecological meltdown is impossible to say. The precautionary principle would have us take no risks and conserve every animal from polar bears to beetles. In fact, we seem likely to lose a high proportion of species during the next century—perhaps 50 percent or more—as human population doubles and the stresses on habitat become even greater than at present.

While the *economic* value of biodiversity is what drives government policy, the *nonmaterialist* benefits should not be underestimated. Nature makes people feel good. That is why we flock to parks, cultivate gardens, and keep pets. Nature has a spiritual value to humanity that is real, even if hard to measure by standard means. Serious loss of natural forests and plant and animal species would greatly decrease our quality of life and spiritual comfort.

The loss of beautiful birds to extinction is not just an aesthetic matter. Birds play a key role in controlling insects, some of

---

The "balance of nature" is not just a romantic phrase. It has real meaning.

---

which (mosquitoes, for example) are important disease carriers. Reductions in migratory bird populations can mean that losses through hunting, habitat disturbance, or pollution in one country can mean insect infestation in another. The "balance of nature" is not just a romantic phrase. It has real meaning. The loss of one animal may trigger other losses in the food chain or lead to an explosion of population among lesser animals, such as rodents or insects.

However, the animals and plants that arouse most affection in people—bears, dolphins, penguins, butterflies, redwood trees, orchids—form only a tiny proportion of Earth's **biomass**. Human beings and all other species could not exist without the millions of smaller species—bacteria, fungi, nematodes, insects, etc.—that support the pyramid of life on Earth. How much damage is being done to these supporting species is hard to say, but most studies find depressing evidence of relentless degradation—loss of soil fertility, widespread contamination of groundwater, polluted air, and so on.

Redwood trees, the subjects of many conservation efforts, are a foundation species, providing critical support to their ecosystem.

Although much effort has gone into harvesting the ocean's wildlife to provide protein for human consumption and fish meal for animals, the oceans remain a largely untapped resource as far as other uses are concerned. Yet the chemical profusion of marine life provides many possibilities for commercial use. Already, marine organisms have provided the source for a range of antibiotics and cancer-treating drugs. We are discovering these possibilities just at the time when advances in chemical and genetic engineering are bringing synthetic production of new drugs, materials, and even life forms. The big companies may decide that controlled, design-driven production makes more sense than struggling through nature to find useful products.

According to Julian Simons, long-time "anti-green," "Recent scientific and technical advances—especially seed banks and genetic engineering—have diminished the importance of maintaining species in their natural habitats." This is a valid point and serves to highlight the need for "greens" to clarify their arguments in favor of general conservation. Yet it must be

---

Flora and fauna produced in a laboratory could not possibly match the genetic variety that nature has already given us.

---

acknowledged that flora and fauna produced in a laboratory could not possibly match the genetic variety that nature has already given us.

Biodiversity is a sign of a healthy and flexible ecosystem. This is true both at the local level and in terms of the whole earth. Conservation of some species is a practical necessity. Conservation of others raises ethical and aesthetic issues—including our responsibility to future generations. Deciding *which* species to conserve is by no means straightforward.

FAUNA AND FLORA THROUGHOUT THE WORLD
(in thousands)

	Known species	Estimated total	
Viruses	4	400	
Bacteria	4	1,000	Bacteria
Fungi	72	1,500	
Protozoa	40	200	
Algae	40	400	
Plants	270	320	
Nematodes	25	400	
Crustaceans	40	150	
Arachnids	75	750	Plants
Insects	950	8,000	
Mollusks	70	200	
Vertebrates	45	50	
Others	115	250	
Total	1,750	13,620	Insects

Source: Global Biodiversity Assessment UNEP, 1995

KEY CONCEPTS

Traditional medicine Health practices, knowledge, and beliefs that involve plant-, animal-, and mineral-based medicines, spiritual therapies, manual techniques, and exercises that are applied to treat and prevent illness, or maintain well-being are considered to be traditional medicine. Twenty-five percent of modern medicines are made from plants first used traditionally. More than 50 percent of the population of **industrialized** nations have used traditional medicine. In most countries, the herbal medicine market is not controlled by regulatory bodies.

KEYSTONE SPECIES

While all species in a habitat depend on each other for survival, some species play a more important role in maintaining the quality of the habitat. If these keystone species are removed or disappear from a habitat, the connection between that species and others in the habitat begins to change. In essence, the delicately balanced system falls apart.

Scientists believe animals such as the California sea otter may be keystone species in an ecosystem. The sea otter is a West Coast mammal that lives on floating kelp beds. Its main food is spiny sea urchins from the ocean floor. Prized for its fur, the sea otter was hunted in the 1700s until it was believed to be extinct. Since otters were no longer eating sea urchins, the sea urchin population soon increased, and the urchins ate kelp until it too was gone.

Kelp beds provide a habitat for many marine creatures. These creatures are food for fish. Kelp also softens the force of waves, keeping the shore from eroding during storms. Some surviving sea otters were found living farther north along the coast. They were brought back to places from which they had disappeared and were protected by the government. The sea urchin had a predator once again. As sea urchin numbers fell, the kelp began to grow. The natural balance in the ecosystem was restored.

Balance of nature In ecological terms, the balance of nature describes natural systems as being in a state of equilibrium or balance, in which disturbing one element disturbs the entire system. In most cases, a variety of things influence the abundance of a species, including predators, food availability, competition with other species, disease, and even the weather. These factors are not constant, but ever-changing. The balance achieved is dynamic, not static. So, in reality, the balance is continually upset by natural events. Modern ecologists question the existence of a balance of nature because the natural state of any system is not necessarily the preferred state.

Forests and Habitat Loss

Until this century, the world had vast areas of forest, wilderness, and coastline that were virtually untouched by human activity. Industrial development was confined to a relatively small number of places. Tourism was small scale. Most of the planet's land surface was the domain of the animal kingdom, and there was relatively little disturbance or pollution of the seas. Damage to the biosphere from human activity was localized or confined to a few species.

In the last 200 years, the human population has exploded, growing from one billion in 1830, to 6.5 billion in 2006, with a further doubling expected in the next century. The Industrial Revolution set in motion a series of human disturbances to the ecosystem that were completely different in scale from what had gone before. As well, for the first time in history, materials were being produced that could not easily be recycled by the natural processes of nature. Intensive agriculture, road networks, mining, and pollution

■■■ **Trees play an important role in the environment by exchanging gases between the biosphere and part of the atmosphere. Deforestation puts much of this at risk.**

contributed to the new burdens thrust upon the biosphere.

It is questionable whether or not the biosphere can support the expected doubling of the human population. Statistics show that about 20 to 50 percent of the world's forest cover has been put to other uses since preagricultural times.

In 2005, the Food and Agriculture Organization of the United Nations (FAO) estimated the world's forest at 10 billion acres (3.9 billion h)—an area the size of North, Central, and South America combined. Natural

---

Taming the wild seems desirable and necessary to poor countries seeking to modernize.

---

forest consisted of 96.2 percent, and forest plantations 3.8 percent. Since 1990, annual forest loss worldwide has been 21.9 million acres (8.9 million h), of which most was natural forest in the tropics.

Forest cover in the richer industrialized nations is more or less stable, although so-called "sustainable" plantations have often replaced natural forest. According to the FAO, in 2001, North American forest cover had

expanded almost 10 million acres (4 million h), but had lost about 12 million acres (5 million h) by 2005. The United States has about the same area of forest as it did in 1920, despite its increase in population. Advances in technology have made it possible to produce more food on the same amount of land.

In the developing world, deforestation continues apace. On the island of Sumatra in Indonesia, it has taken 25 years to destroy all lowland forests with their native faunas. Sumatra is about the size of England.

The English countryside is often admired for its beauty, but it had a very different appearance in the Middle Ages, before the great oak forests were cut down—together with much of the wildlife that used to inhabit them. Bears and wolves in Britain were hunted out of existence many centuries ago. As in other mature industrial nations, nature has been largely domesticated in Great Britain. The developing world is now busily engaged in making the same transformation. Taming the wild seems desirable and necessary to poor countries seeking to modernize. Rich countries that urge them to conserve their jungles and swamps are accused of hypocrisy.

In Southeast Asia, in Latin America, and in central Africa, the story is the same—the rain forest is diminishing as farmers and loggers take their toll. Plantation growth, a major feature of forests in **temperate** regions, is taking hold in some **tropical** areas. The problem with this is that the planting of eucalyptus or other alien fast-growing trees over large areas is not likely to contribute to biodiversity—quite the contrary. The emphasis on specialized plants diminishes the diversity on Earth.

Mangroves are one of Earth's most productive and diverse habitats. Unfortunately, they are among its most threatened. According to the International Tropical Timber Organization (ITTO), in 2003 mangrove forests occupied about 42 million acres (17 million h) of tropical coast worldwide. Presently, these forests are disappearing at a rate of about

---

There is still no international agreement on how to protect the world's forests.

247,000 acres (100,000 h) each year. The World Wildlife Fund (WWF) estimates about 35 percent of the world's mangroves are already gone. Occasionally, a change is seen in this trend. In an area of Thailand called Phuket, the mangroves are

expanding since the area's tin mines were abandoned.

Many other ecosystems are being damaged or destroyed by human activity, either as a result of economic development, including new dams, roads, mines, logging, and cattle ranches, or subsistence agriculture in the form of poor farmers nibbling away at the edges of forests, often using "slash and burn" methods. Poverty, population growth, and economic development all contribute to deforestation and other forms of habitat destruction.

There is still no international agreement on how to protect the world's forests, though an Intergovernmental Panel on Forests, set up in 1994, may

CHANGES IN FOREST COVER, 2000-2005

Continent	Total Forest in 2000	Total Forest in 2005	Change 2000-2005
	Thousand Acres (Hectares)		Percentage
Africa	1,620,055 (655,613)	1,570,137 (635,412)	-0.62
Asia	1,400,005 (566,562)	1,412,398 (571,577)	0.18
Oceania	514,063 (208,034)	509,665 (206,254)	-0.17
Europe	2,466,337 (998,091)	2,474,498 (1,001,394)	0.07
North & Central America	1,748,305 (707,514)	1,744,191 (831,540)	-0.05
South America	2,107,305 (852,796)	2,054,780 (831,540)	-0.50
Total World	9,856,070 (3,988,610)	9,765,666 (3,952,025)	-0.18

Source: Global Forest Resources Assessment, 2005, FAO

succeed in setting new standards. Under targets set by the 1994 International Tropical Timber Agreement (ITTA), all tropical forest products were supposed to come from sustainably managed forests by the year 2000. Though Year 2000 Objective is nonbinding and vague, it at least shows that rain forest protection is being taken seriously at the international level. The goal of Year 2000 Objective was not achieved, but work is continuing to meet this challenge.

The assumption that **clear-cut logging** is the only cost-effective way to harvest forest resources is gradually being replaced with a more sophisticated, "sustainable" approach. To protect rain forests, extract the resources from that specific area. Everything else in the area is left untouched. The involvement of local people in running extractive reserves offers the prospect of combining a decent economic return from **ecotourism,** with conservation of biodiversity. This is the dilemma—how to balance the desire to preserve natural biodiversity with the need to improve living standards for billions of people.

▬▬ **Mangroves preserve water quality and diminish pollution by filtering substances in water.**

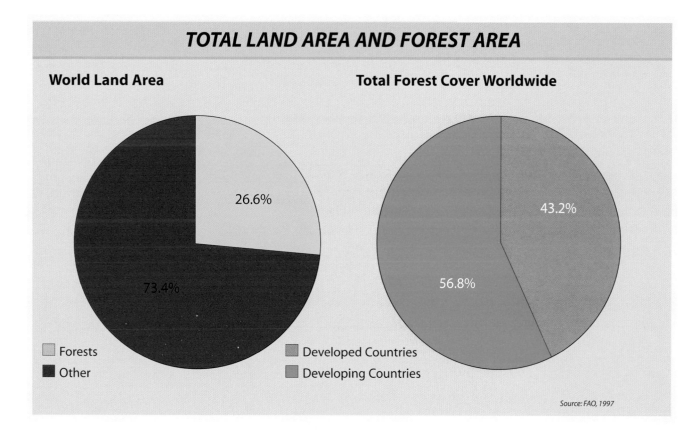

TOTAL LAND AREA AND FOREST AREA

World Land Area

26.6%

73.4%

- ☐ Forests
- ■ Other

Total Forest Cover Worldwide

43.2%

56.8%

- ▨ Developed Countries
- ▨ Developing Countries

Source: FAO, 1997

WHAT FORESTS PROVIDE

Forests are storage rooms of biodiversity. As living systems, they play a vital role in fulfilling the physical, social, and cultural needs of humans.

Food
Uses: food products to grow and eat
Examples: seeds, nuts, roots, tubers, mushrooms, fruits, saps, gums, oils

Medicines
Uses: prescription drugs, traditional plant remedies
Examples: teas, herbs

Fiber
Uses: furniture, clothing
Examples: rattan, jute, bamboo

Essences
Uses: perfumes, cosmetics
Examples: herbs, gums, saps, resins, syrups

Fertilizers
Uses: soil nourishment
Examples: compost, nitrogen

Recreation
Uses: tourism, relaxation, sporting activities
Examples: parks, wildlife reserves

Fuel
Uses: warming buildings
Examples: wood, charcoal

Timber products
Uses: construction, paper products
Examples: lumber, pulp

KEY CONCEPTS

Deforestation Forests are cut down for forest products, or to clear land for agriculture, construction, or other human activities.

Intensive agriculture Intensive farming methods allow a relatively small number of people to produce vast quantities of food. Energy, money, and production methods are concentrated on a particular crop of animal. Technology, in the form of chemicals, genetic engineering, and hormones, is used to maximize output. Intensive farming is highly efficient in the short term, producing as much food as possible as cheaply as possible.

Subsistence agriculture Subsistence agriculture is small-scale farming whereby farmers grow only enough crops to keep their families alive. When a population is large, subsistence agriculture can cause serious deforestation.

Sustainable development Sustainable management of ecosystems is a form of development that meets the needs of present generations while also considering the needs of future generations. Putting sustainable development into practice requires making difficult political decisions. It involves rethinking how money is earned and used.

Duties: Work to change attitudes toward the environment through public education

Education: Bachelor of science degree in environmental science or a related discipline

Interests: Environmental protection, public education, public speaking, and a passion for the environment

To learn more about a career as an environmentalist, navigate to **www.princetonreview.com/cte/ profiles/dayInLife.asp?careerID =61**. Also click on **http:// investigate.conservation.org/xp /IB/conservationcareers/career _options.xml** to explore more environmentally-oriented careers.

Careers in Focus

Environmentalists strive to protect biodiversity. They provide information to the public that helps people make informed decisions about the use of limited natural resources. Environmentalists work for **nongovernmental organizations** (NGOs), organize people at the grassroots level, and advise governments on environmental policy issues. They research, write reports and articles, lecture, issue press releases, lobby politicians, fund raise, and campaign.

Most environmentalists specialize in a particular field. Some environmentalists work for companies that sell environmentally friendly goods and services, but most work for nonprofit environmental organizations. Some positions involve office work, policy analysis, lab work, or computer analysis. Other environmentalists work outdoors more, where they measure the speed and pattern of environmental decay, including examining the depletion of the ozone layer, contaminated groundwater in suburban communities, and the destruction of animal habitat.

While formal education is not required, many environmentalists hold a bachelor of science degree in environmental science. Environmentalists need critical-thinking skills to analyze environmental issues and scientific data. Many environmentalists work long hours for little pay, but they get satisfaction from knowing that their work makes a difference in the health of the planet.

Hunting and Invading

There are many examples of wild animals being hunted to near extinction. Examples include the North American buffalo, the blue whale, the panda, the gorilla, and the tiger. Our ancestors managed to wipe out the megafauna, such as giant kangaroos and mammoths, that once roamed in Australia, the Americas, and Europe. Large flightless birds were quickly eliminated by settlers in the Pacific islands.

Hunting still has a strong cultural appeal in many countries. Aboriginal populations are allowed limited hunting of polar bears in Russia and Alaska. Presently,

> *There are many examples of wild animals being hunted to the edge of collapse or even extinction.*

many groups of people also hunt polar bears illegally, which is seriously reducing the population. In Italy, wild birds are slaughtered in their millions when the spring hunting season opens. Hunting of primates for food has been an accepted practice by Aboriginal cultures for centuries. This poses a significant threat to the continued existence of monkeys and apes. The World Wildlife Fund anticipates that if excessive hunting practices continue, by the year 2025, Earth could lose as many as 20 percent of all species known to exist today.

The U.S. big game clubs want to hunt limited numbers of gorillas, tigers, rhinos, and

The United States Marine Mammal Protection Act is one piece of legislation that protects the polar bear.

leopards, arguing that this gives hunters a stake in the conservation of wild species. Some hunting organizations in the United States maintain they put the majority of their funds into wildlife conservation. Similar proposals have been made on the reintroduction of a limited trade in ivory "in order to protect elephants." The "use it or lose it" argument is one of the most fiercely debated issues in modern conservation. Those favoring controlled use might say, for example, that pheasants are in plentiful supply in Great Britain because a handful of people enjoy the sport of pheasant shooting.

In the 20th century, the biggest instance of overhunting has been the harvesting of the oceans. The rich biodiversity of the seas has been hit hard by the development of commercial fishing techniques—factory ships, shrimp trawlers, drift nets, and so on. The global fish catch of marine species was about 90 million tons (81.65 million t) in 2005. It has been at about that level for over a decade. Many traditional species have been greatly overexploited, and attention has switched to smaller fish and new species.

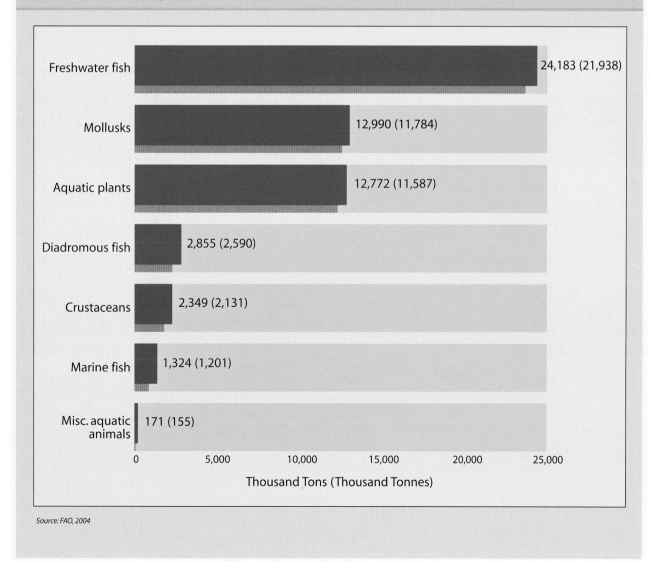

WORLD AQUACULTURE PRODUCTION: MAJOR SPECIES 2002

Freshwater fish — 24,183 (21,938)
Mollusks — 12,990 (11,784)
Aquatic plants — 12,772 (11,587)
Diadromous fish — 2,855 (2,590)
Crustaceans — 2,349 (2,131)
Marine fish — 1,324 (1,201)
Misc. aquatic animals — 171 (155)

Thousand Tons (Thousand Tonnes)

Source: FAO, 2004

Not that we are the only species to indulge in overkill when we arrive as strangers in a new habitat. The rabbit, brought to Australia in 1859, soon overran that vast country, affecting ecosystems throughout the nation. Brown tree snakes introduced from Papua New Guinea have had a severe impact on the bird population of Guam. Ship-borne rats and cats have done the same for many other island populations of birds and small mammals.

Islands and their aquatic counterparts, fresh- or saltwater lakes, are particularly vulnerable to species extinctions, yet they are often home to many original species that cannot be found anywhere else. The Galapagos Islands provide the most famous

---

Islands and their aquatic counterparts, fresh- or saltwater lakes, are particularly vulnerable to species extinctions.

---

example of island endemism. This island featured prominently in Charles Darwin's *Origin of Species*.

Africa's Lake Victoria, once home to over 350 varieties of fish, now holds half that number. This is owing to a combination of overfishing and the predatory behavior of the Nile perch, a large protein-rich species introduced to boost fish stocks. Introductions of a fish called tilapia have damaged fish diversity in the lakes and rivers of many other countries. "Homogenized" farm salmon are interbreeding with wild salmon, reducing the genetic variety that enabled different salmon to adapt to local river conditions. Worldwide, a third of freshwater fish species are at risk of extinction.

THE EXTINCTION OF THE AMERICAN PASSENGER PIGEON

The story of the fate of the American passenger pigeon reads like a romance. When the Europeans settled in North America, it is thought that that there were about five billion passenger pigeons on the continent. This would have been about one-third of all the birds in North America at the time. When the pigeons migrated, it took days for the huge mass of birds to pass an area. They would fly in large, continuous flocks for hours at a time.

The passenger pigeon existed in such large numbers because there was a lack of natural predators. Once human intervention occurred, they were surprisingly vulnerable. As the human population increased in North America in the 19th century, the passenger pigeon was considered a source of cheap meat. Hundreds of thousands of the birds were killed weekly. Each female laid only one egg a year, so it was difficult to replace any losses quickly. It took only about 100 years to decimate their population. The last surviving passenger pigeon known to exist on Earth died at the Cincinnati Zoo in 1914, marking the end of a species.

The zebra mussel, native to the Caspian Sea, is damaging the Great Lakes of North America. The U.S. comb jellyfish has colonized the Black Sea, outcompeting local marine species already threatened by algae buildup.

Livestock farming can also threaten local biodiversity through competition for food or the introduction of new diseases. Rinderpest, a deadly infectious disease that struck down the ungulate population of Africa in the 1890s, was one notorious example.

Just as dramatic can be the effect of alien species of plant.

The prolific South American water hyacinth has come to dominate plant growth in parts of Africa and China, where it also blocks irrigation canals, dam

---

A new threat is the introduction into the environment of living modified organisms.

---

turbines, and water pipes. Asian cheat grass is spreading in North America, replacing traditional plants. At least 50 percent of weed varieties and some 40

percent of insect pests in the United States are exotic species. Meanwhile, the large-scale dumping of **ballast water** by ships is disturbing marine ecosystems worldwide.

A new threat to Earth is the introduction into the environment of living modified organisms, or the products of genetic engineering—a problem that the Convention on Biological Diversity tried to address through its proposal for a "Biosafety Protocol." Such introductions are irreversible and very risky.

NUMBER OF THREATENED ANIMAL SPECIES

Vertebrates	1996/98	2000	2004
Mammals	1,096	1,130	1,101
Birds	1,107	1,183	1,213
Amphibians	124	146	1,856
Reptiles	253	296	304
Fishes	734	752	800
Subtotal	**3,314**	**3,507**	**5,274**

Invertebrates	1996/98	2000	2004
Insects	537	555	559
Mollusks	920	938	974
Crustaceans	407	408	429
Other Inverts	27	27	30
Subtotal	**1,891**	**1,928**	**1,992**

Source: World Conservation Union (IUCN)

■■■ The International Whaling Commission was established in 1946 to oversee worldwide whaling so that the conservation of whale stocks is ensured.

KEY CONCEPTS

Conservation bodies Concern for marine conservation has spawned the growth of numerous intergovernmental bodies and nongovernmental organizations during the past 20 years. One such organization is the International Whaling Commission (IWC). The Marine Stewardship Council (MSC), which certifies sustainable fisheries, is another example. None of these bodies has much more than advisory power, however.

Careers in Focus

Wildlife officers protect biodiversity by enforcing fish and wildlife laws and administering conservation programs. In the United States, most wildlife officers work for state governments, but some work for the federal government as special agents. To become a wildlife officer, a candidate must pass tests in a number of subjects, including the principles of law enforcement, conservation, ecology, and the habits and distribution of wildlife in their area. These tests vary from state to state. In addition, prospective wildlife officers must pass a physical exam and an endurance test.

Wildlife officers work outdoors patrolling parks, coastlines, and recreational areas. They issue warnings and citations and arrest people suspected of poaching and other wildlife violations. They also investigate coastal pollution and illegal commercial fishing operations. Wildlife officers pursue and detain people suspected of wildlife crimes. They will seize equipment, fish, and wildlife from suspects.

Wildlife officers work on research and public education initiatives developing conservation programs. Officers ensure that species are not overhunted, or are too numerous in a particular area. They also investigate crop damage caused by wildlife and advise landowners of possible preventative measures. This ensures the biodiversity of the area is maintained. Wildlife officers provide conservation education, speaking at public events and in classrooms, and educating hunters about safety and wildlife laws.

Trade and Cultural Loss

Global trade has both direct and indirect effects on biodiversity. If people live and work in a small community directly dependent on the land, they learn to work in harmony with nature, aware of the interaction of plants, animals, weather, and seasons. A society based on specialized trade blurs these links. Seasons have no impact, and animals and plants become unknown occupants of an unseen conveyor belt that leads to mass-produced food and other products.

Global trade breaks the link between land and community. Few city residents have any real notion of how their food is produced. Abuse of the environment is carried out at a distance, its results seemingly unconnected with daily life. There is no going back, of course. Returning to universal subsistence farming would be absurd. If "sustainable development" is to be an achievable goal, humanity needs to recover a strong awareness of nature's basic laws.

World output of goods and services increased from $7 trillion in 1950 to $56 trillion in 2004. While this has helped to raise living standards, it has also increased stresses on the environment. More international trade means higher energy use, more roads for transport, and, because goods have to be packaged for shipment, more waste. More packaging increases the demand for paper products, which adds to the pressure on forests and natural habitats. Few seriously advocate an end to

---

More international trade means higher energy use, more roads for transport, and more waste.

---

international trade, but a more responsible, "ecoaware" approach is certainly needed.

A more direct result of trade is the buying and selling of wildlife products, ranging from ivory to turtle eggs. This business is worth some $20 billion a year, according to the WWF.

The Convention on International Trade in Endangered Species (CITES) attempts to regulate trade in endangered species. Though CITES has helped to limit wildlife trade, ivory being the most prominent example, illegal trading is widespread. Bear bile, tiger bones, shark's fins, rhino and antelope horn are the ingredients of many oriental remedies. The demand for exotic foods and traditional medicines is strong, and the diminishing jungles of Southeast Asia, such as Myanmar, Cambodia, Laos, Thailand, and Indonesia, bear the main brunt of hunting efforts. The military dictatorship of Myanmar is not party to CITES and pays little attention to conservation of wildlife. The jungles are ruthlessly cleared of both animal populations that stand in the way of "free market" development.

The recent outbreak of the disease Severe Acute Respiratory Syndrome (SARS) in Asia, as well as concern about the spread of avian flu, has brought the issue of wildlife trade to world attention. Like humans and other species, birds are susceptible to flu. Bird flu was thought only to infect birds until the first human cases were seen in Hong Kong in 1997. The type of greatest concern is the deadly strain H5N1, which can prove fatal to humans. Humans catch the disease through close contact with live, infected birds. As of April 2006, the World Health Organization (WHO) had confirmed 204 cases of H5N1 in humans, leading to 113 deaths.

■ To prevent the illegal trade of ivory, tusks seized by authorities are often set on fire and destroyed.

Rapid economic development, greed, corruption, and poverty are the enemies of biodiversity. Wildlife, caught between deforestation, poaching, and large-scale construction projects, is running out of room. In Indonesia, for example, the government is keen to develop Sumatra to take pressure off the overcrowded island of Java. The Sumatran forests are home to many species of plants and animals, many of them unique to the area. A Sumatran tiger may be sold by a poacher for less than $200. Middlemen and retailers then chalk up the price tenfold. If only the buyers could be persuaded to change their habits. If only the hunter—with his homemade gun and clever trapping systems—could earn his $200 in a less destructive way. Somehow, market forces need to be geared to the conservation of species and not their obliteration.

Unfortunately, the problem of poverty among the people who live closest to wildlife areas, combined with the demand for wildlife products in both developing and developed worlds, makes legal protection more of a soothing response to public opinion than an effective measure. Tiger hunting has been against international law for years, but that has not stopped the business of killing and trading in tigers. Legal measures have to be strongly enforced and backed by socio-economic measures that remove the incentive to cut down

---

Rapid economic development, greed, corruption, and poverty are the enemies of biodiversity.

---

primary forest and hunt rare wildlife. This is much easier said than done.

Many undeveloped parts of the world are still inhabited not only by rare animals, but also by indigenous tribal groups. It is finally dawning on the outside world that the detailed knowledge of plants and animals that such groups have built up over the centuries is valuable—and irreplaceable. One scientific study of the rain forest in Amazonia identified 295 different tree species in a sample area. The local Yanomami Indians had names for them all and separate uses for 280 of the species found. Such examples could be repeated for indigenous groups all over the world.

This knowledge, along with the local languages that pass it down, is vanishing rapidly under the advancing tide of civilization. Some indigenous groups, in countries such as Australia, Brazil, and Colombia, have won important legal rights to compensation and have learned to use modern technology, including the Internet, to support their cause. Few have won the right to live undisturbed on their ancestral lands. Ethnobotany—the study of the interaction between people and plants—is at last taken seriously in the West, but much ethnic knowledge of nature has already been lost. "Primitive" tribes stand little chance against modernizing governments. Oil company operations, dam-building projects, and the construction of roads and power stations have caused damage both to wildlife and tribal groups. Whether this "price of progress" is worth paying depends on your point of view.

KEY CONCEPTS

Ethnobotany Ethnobotany aims to study how and why people use plants in their local environments. The plant lore and agricultural customs of a people are examined, but the emphasis is on the medicinal uses of plants. As well, ethnobotanists explore the lives of the people that live around them and use them.

ENDANGERED TIGERS

Three tiger subspecies—the Bali, Javan, and Caspian—have become extinct in the past 70 years. The five remaining subspecies—Amur, Bengal, Indochinese, South China, and Sumatran—live only in Asia, and all are threatened by poaching and habitat loss.

Bengal Tiger

- The estimated wild population of Bengal tigers is approximately 3,100-4,700 tigers. About 333 live in captivity, primarily in zoos in India.
- Most Bengal tigers live in India, although some range through Nepal, Bangladesh, Bhutan, and Myanmar.

Sumatran Tiger

- About 400 wild Sumatran tigers are believed to exist—primarily in Sumatra's five national parks—and 210 captive animals live in zoos around the world.
- In nature, the Sumatran tiger is found only on the Indonesian island of Sumatra in habitat that ranges from lowland forest to submontane and montane forest.

Amur/Siberian Tiger

- It is estimated that 360-406 Amur, or Siberian, tigers still exist in the wild. About 490 captive Amur tigers are managed in zoo conservation programs.
- The Amur tiger lives primarily in the coniferous, scrub oak, and birch woodlands of eastern Russia, with a few found in northeastern China and northern North Korea.

Indochinese Tiger

- An estimated 1,200-1,800 Indochinese tigers are left in the wild, and about 60 live in zoos in Asia and the United States.
- The distribution of the Indochinese tiger is centered in Thailand. Indochinese tigers are also found in Myanmar, southern China, Cambodia, Laos, Vietnam, and peninsular Malaysia.

South China Tiger

- It is estimated that, at most, only 20-30 South China tigers still exist in the wild. Currently 47 South China tigers live in 18 zoos, all in China. The South China tiger is the most critically endangered of all tiger subspecies.

Mapping the World's Largest Protected Areas

Greenland (DENMARK)

Alaska (U.S.)

CANADA

UNITED STATES

Hawai'i (U.S.)

MEXICO

BAHAMAS

CUBA

DOMINICAN REPUBLIC

Puerto Rico (U.S.)

HAITI

JAMAICA

BELIZE

ANTIGUA AND BARBUDA

ST. KITTS AND NEVIS

DOMINICA

GUATEMALA

HONDURAS

ST. LUCIA

EL SALVADOR

NICARAGUA

ST. VINCENT AND THE GRENADINES

BARBADOS

GRENADA

COSTA RICA

PANAMA

TRINIDAD AND TOBAGO

VENEZUELA

GUYANA

SURINAME

COLOMBIA

French Guiana (FRANCE)

Galápagos Islands (ECUADOR)

ECUADOR

PERU

BRAZIL

BOLIVIA

PARAGUAY

CHILE

URUGUAY

ARGENTINA

Falkland Islands (U.K.)

Protected areas by country
(% of total land area)

	0–5
	5–10
	10–15
	15–20
	20–25
	Over 25
	No information available

N

SCALE AT EQUATOR

0   1,000   2,000   3,000 miles

0   1,609   3,219   4,828 kilometers

Figure 1: The World's 20 Largest Protected Areas

More than 100,000 protected areas have been established across the developed and developing worlds in an effort to conserve the world's most spectacular habitats and wildlife. Over 7 million square miles (18 million sq km) benefit from protected area status. These range in size from 375 million square miles (972,000 sq km) to 4 square miles (10 sq km).

Source: UN Environment Programme, World Conservation Monitoring Centre

Charting Habitats and Biodiversity

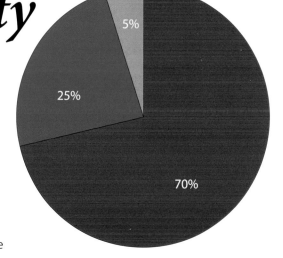

Figure 2: Expansion and Contraction of Agriculture and Forests, 2002

The FAO examines the relationship between forested and agricultural areas. Findings show that agricultural land is expanding in about 70 percent of countries, declining in 25 percent, and staying the same in 5 percent.

- Agriculture Expanding
- Agriculture Contracting
- Agriculture Stable

Figure 3: Countries with the Greatest Biodiversity

Countries found in or near tropical rain forests hold the greatest number of plant and animal species.

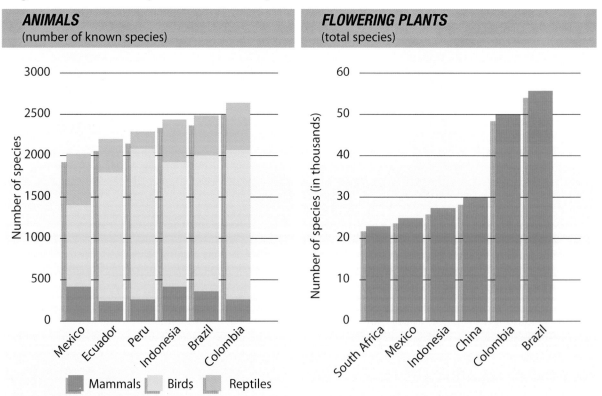

ANIMALS (number of known species)

FLOWERING PLANTS (total species)

Mammals   Birds   Reptiles

Source: UNEP, World Conservation Monitoring Centre

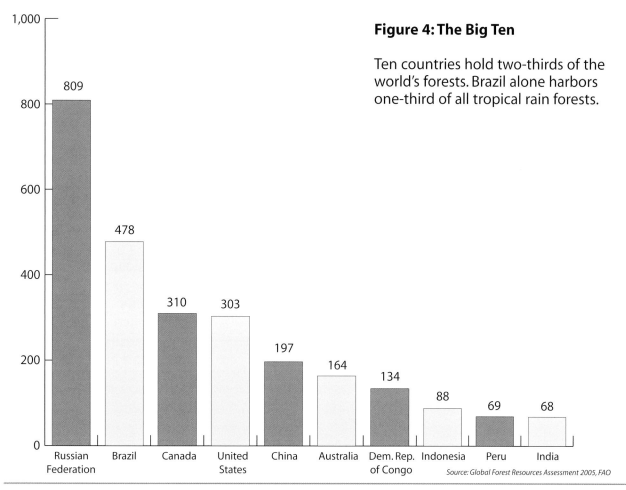

Figure 4: The Big Ten

Ten countries hold two-thirds of the world's forests. Brazil alone harbors one-third of all tropical rain forests.

Bar chart values:
- Russian Federation: 809
- Brazil: 478
- Canada: 310
- United States: 303
- China: 197
- Australia: 164
- Dem. Rep. of Congo: 134
- Indonesia: 88
- Peru: 69
- India: 68

Source: Global Forest Resources Assessment 2005, FAO

Figure 5: Trade in Live Primates Legal Exports and Imports 2002, World Resources Institute

Live primate exports and imports include monkeys, apes, and prosimians (for example, lemurs). These figures are based on permits issued and not on actual primates traded.

Exports		Imports	
Barbados	1,542	Australia	266
China	14,322	Belgium	1,135
Guyana	918	Canada	1,209
Indonesia	3,250	France	3,373
Mauritius	7,299	Great Britain	2,266
Philippines	2,654	Germany	705
Saint Kitts & Nevis	380	Japan	5,978
South Africa	678	Netherlands	819
Tanzania	844	Serbia & Montenegro	550
Vietnam	5,142	Thailand	310
		United States	19,530

Paths of Destruction

Ecologically-positive people, or ecooptimist, claim that advanced agricultural technology will soon be available to provide enough food for 10 or even 15 billion people without increasing cropland areas by more than a few percentage points. It is said that fast-growing plantation forests can provide enough wood for timber and paper pulp needs without destroying the rain forest. Aquaculture, they say, already accounts for 27 percent of global fish catch and can easily be developed further to ensure that fish supplies remain plentiful.

Economic growth cannot be achieved without an environmental downside.

Others, less hopeful, point out that even with 6.5 billion people, the stresses on the natural world have become almost impossible. The evidence for distress is plain to see—the ozone hole, depletion of fish stocks, more areas becoming deserts, soil erosion, more areas becoming salty, pollution, the endless buildup of toxic waste, water shortages and contamination, new diseases, and so on. Responsibility for all this lies mainly with the rich industrialized nations. As

green organizations regularly state, the rich nations account for 20 percent of world population, but 85 percent of world pollution. It seems obvious that doubling the size of the world's population will greatly increase the scale of environmental destruction.

Some hope can be taken from the fact that the rich nations now pay serious attention to green issues. Higher living standards bring a desire to breathe cleaner air, drink purer water, get rid of smelly waste, and conserve nature. On the one hand, wealth provides the means to develop new technologies to clean up the

Large reservoirs, such as the Three Gorges Dam Reservoir in China, can generate sizable quantities of greenhouse gases due to the high concentration of microorganisms living within the habitat.

environment. On the other hand, it is also true that wealthy nations can afford to transfer the burden of the pollution they cause into someone else's backyard. Japan conserves its own forests while importing large amounts of tropical timber from poorer countries. The Netherlands has strict conservation laws to protect its own wildlife, but is a major importer of exotic wild birds, mainly from tropical forest regions.

Economic growth cannot be achieved without an environmental downside. Some degree of damage is inevitable; how much will depend more on political will than technology. However, techno-fix solutions may have unfortunate side-effects, too. Large-scale aquaculture, for example, involves the heavy use of grain feedstuffs, substantial waste generation, and an increased risk of disease or pesticide contamination. Intensive production, whether of trees, grain, fish, or livestock, puts an enormous strain on natural ecosystems.

Until recently, most oil industry production was done in desert areas, supposedly devoid of life. Development in biodiverse areas, such as

Colombia, Sumatra, and Nigeria, has caused far more fuss. The dams that were built by rich countries in the name of progress earlier in this century aroused little opposition on the grounds of environmental destruction. Safely in possession of plentiful electricity and water, the citizens of rich countries now frown upon similar development projects in other parts of the world. "Learn from our past mistakes," the rich countries urge.

Sadly, the biggest expansions of population and the most urgent demands for energy, food, water, and industrial products are in countries with the greatest remaining biodiversity. We want to delay harmful development with environmental impact assessments. They want to escape from poverty as soon as possible, and that means putting humans before animals and trees.

The richest marine biodiversity appears to be around the western Pacific islands and in the Indian Ocean—next to the most heavily populated and fastest-developing regions of the world. Coral reefs, fragile homes to the greatest marine diversity of all, are being damaged at a terrifying rate. Globally, 60 percent of the world's reefs are at risk from human activities, with about 27 percent of reefs at high or very high risk. In late 2000, the Global Coral Reef Monitoring Network (GCRMN) assessed the loss of the world's reefs at 28 percent.

The accumulation of such disturbances could eventually lead to some kind of ecosystem collapse, making the planet unfriendly to humans. This may not be as far-fetched as it sounds. There has already been damage to every part of the globe from polar icecaps to the ocean deeps. Atmosphere, water, and climate have all been affected by human activity. It remains to be seen if unsustainable living will ruin Earth entirely.

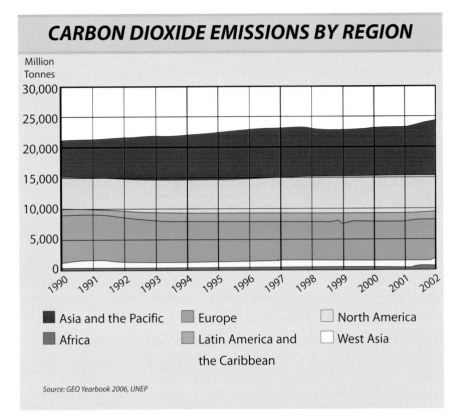

CARBON DIOXIDE EMISSIONS BY REGION

Million Tonnes

Legend:
- Asia and the Pacific
- Africa
- Europe
- Latin America and the Caribbean
- North America
- West Asia

Source: GEO Yearbook 2006, UNEP

Coral reefs have been called the "rain forests of the sea," referring to the great biodiversity of both reefs and rain forests.

ACCOUNTING FOR THE ENVIRONMENT: THE PROBLEM OF EXTERNAL COSTS

The present System of National Accounts (SNA), devised as part of the global economic framework put in place after World War II, uses **gross domestic product** (GDP) as the way to measure a country's prosperity. GDP depends entirely on economic activity. Whereas a company's balance sheet and profit and loss account show both the net asset value of the business and its profitability over a period, GDP takes no account of assets, depreciation, or contingent liabilities, such as an aging population. Quality of life does not come into the picture. Measurement by GDP can produce strange results. A natural catastrophe, which causes major reconstruction, shows up as an increase in GDP and therefore national income. The short-term income generated by depletion of a national resource, such as a forest or mineral reserve, also boosts GDP, despite the long-term impact on national wealth.

The costs of environmental damage—pollution of air, land and water, acid rain, waste disposal, etc.—are routinely excluded from the costs of the manufacturing processes and end products that cause them. Attempts to make the polluter pay have often snagged on the problem of defining and allocating costs. In other words, present accounting methods encourage the belief that environmental degradation can be left out of the calculations when economic policy and business decisions are made. The result is a system that works against the best interests of mankind.

Many economists have grappled with this problem and have tried to come up with "green accounting systems." In the early 1990s, the United Nations Statistical Division proposed a new accounting framework called the Integrated System of Environmental and

■■■ **Some forms of pollution are thought to be a main cause of health problems, which become a major economic cost to many citizens and governments worldwide.**

Economic Accounts (IEEA). The hope is that this system will eventually replace the traditional GDP methodology. Another proposal is for green indicators such as ecodomestic product (EDP)—an environmentally adjusted measure of GDP.

The technical problems of introducing green accounting systems are considerable, but not insurmountable—if the will to do it is strong enough. The existing SNA leads governments to "steer with the wrong compass" and therefore continue down the road of unsustainability. The introduction of green accounting could make a big contribution to saving the natural world.

CORAL BLEACHING CAUSE AND EFFECT

The health of the world's coral reefs has been declining over the past several decades. Coral bleaching, which is the discoloration of the coral by the loss of the algae, is one of the main problems facing the reefs. The coral colony becomes stark white or pale in color, showing the underlying white calcium carbonate skeleton.

Recent research indicates that the cause of the bleaching may be caused by global warming, which is producing unusually warm waters. High temperature also weakens coral's ability to fight diseases and grow.

It is difficult for bleached coral to recover. Reefs that are even partly bleached for long periods often die. Dead reefs are vulnerable to waves and other reef skeletons that bore into coral skeletons. This can lead to the reefs breaking up and eroding.

In 1998, there was a significant coral bleaching event that ruined parts of the Indian Ocean, Southeast Asia, and the far western Pacific. Many areas had coral losses of 60–95 percent. The bleaching occurred because of calm conditions during the 1997–98 El Niño–La Niña events, combined with steadily rising baseline sea surface temperatures in the tropics. It could take 20 to 50 years before these coral reefs recover to the level they were at before the bleaching. The recovery may depend on the reduction of human pressures, in the form of global warming, through sound management.

KEY CONCEPTS

Aquaculture Aquaculture is the farming of aquatic organisms, including mollusks, crustaceans, and aquatic plants. Farming implies involvement in the rearing process to improve production, such as regular restocking, feeding, and protection from predators. Some examples of aquaculture include raising catfish in freshwater ponds, growing cultured pearls, and farming salmon in ocean net-pens. Recently, there has been considerable debate on the merits of aquaculture. There are concerns about pollution from fish water and uneaten food, escapees, chemicals to control disease and parasites, and the ecological impacts of sourcing raw materials from the sea to produce fish. When the fish and nonfish species have grown to maturity, they are sold to seafood processors, fish wholesalers, retail fish markets, consumers, pet food manufacturers, and other fish farms as breeding stock.

Coral reefs Corals are animals that form colonies in shallow tropical waters. A collection of such colonies is called a coral reef. Phytoplankton live among the corals, providing oxygen and food. Rich in biodiversity, coral reefs provide fishers with a stable supply of fish to harvest. Today, pollution, nutrient runoff, silt carried into the water because of deforestation, and overfishing are destroying coral reefs on a global scale. According to estimates, 90 percent of coral reefs in the Philippines are either dead or dying.

Born: July 12, 1904, in
Kilternan, Ireland
Died: April 26, 2003
Legacy: Helped to found
a number of important
environmental organizations

For more information, navigate to
Max Nicholson's tribute page at
www.maxnicholson.com.
Or visit The World Conservation
Union press release Web site,
**www.iucn.org/info_and_news/
press/nicholsonmax.pdf**

People in Focus

Max Nicholson was interested in the natural world from an early age. As a child he was an avid bird-watcher and published his first book on birds at the age of 21. He studied history at Oxford and worked in public policy, but after World War II, he switched careers and became a professional conservationist. Nicholson understood the importance of the then new science of ecology and dedicated his conservation efforts to protecting entire ecosystems. Nicholson has been described as a "catalyst for conservation."

Throughout his career, Nicholson founded many organizations dedicated to environmental research and protection. In 1947, he helped form the International Union for the Protection of Nature, now The World Conservation Union. In 1949, he oversaw the founding of The Nature Conservancy. This organization mobilized for legal protection of nature reserves and sites of special scientific interest. In 1961, Nicholson helped to found the World Wildlife Fund (WWF). The WWF helped to convince governments that wildlife and ecosystem protection needed action. He also helped found the International Institute for Environment and Development, Earthwatch Institute, and the British Trust for Ornithology.

Max Nicholson felt it was important to have a solid scientific background when examining ecological issues. He sought to create a scientific database about the world's key conservation areas. Nicholson's efforts as a conservationist and an administrator helped to build many important organizations that continue to work toward the conservation of biodiversity today.

Avenues of Hope

Early attempts to put a stop to species loss focused on the creation of national parks and nature reserves. The number of protected areas is growing, but the setting aside of large natural reserves is only affordable to most countries if they can get some economic return. Ecotourism is one way to bring in foreign currency while protecting wildlife. The difficulty with ecotourism is that the increased number of wealthy visitors, wanting showers, air-conditioned rooms, and three meals a day, brings new stresses to the local environment.

The Judeo-Christian belief that man is at the center of the universe and has dominion over all of Earth and every living thing has had much to do with the Western world view of economic development and material progress. The Christian tradition, like Islam, also consists of the notion of stewardship of Earth—man's responsibility to look after the world that God has created. Hinduism, Taoism, and Buddhism all emphasize the oneness of nature and man's obligation to live in harmony with other creatures. The Jain

monks of India take respect for nature so seriously that they sweep the path as they walk so as to avoid stepping on insects. This might seem extreme to non-Jains, but it is a more harmonious approach to nature than intensive chicken farming. If mankind is to avoid the worst outcomes of a planet-wide

---

They have agreed to protect endangered species of plants and animals and not to use them in unsustainable ways.

---

consumer society, cultural leanings in favor of conservation and respect for wild creatures will have to be considered.

The United States, as the ultimate example of a consumer society, the most powerful nation on Earth, and the biggest user of the world's natural resources, has a special responsibility. The United States has a strong green movement, yet there are many people who oppose the environmental movement. They feel nature should not be a concern before the interests of business, jobs, and people.

The damage to the natural environment demonstrates that the aims of conservation need to be absorbed with those of people who take economic progress for granted.

More than 180 countries have signed up to the Convention on Biological Diversity, which came into force in 1993. Not only have they agreed to protect endangered species of plants and animals and not to use them in unsustainable ways; they have also agreed to the "fair and equitable sharing" of genetic resources. This is a crucial step forward, if it can be applied effectively.

Genetic engineering now brings the possibility that plant and animal species can be conserved in new ways. Synthetic products based on plant genes may make it unnecessary to continue the large-scale collection of plants from the wild. Man is now so dominant on Earth, and so numerous, that even the most remote areas of the planet are touched by human activity. We are gradually taming the wild in one way or another, but that does not necessarily destroy biodiversity. It depends on how we treat the plants and animals under our control.

▬ Hikers are just some of the people who use the 651 acres (263 hectares) of protected land in Oregon's Smith Rock State Park for recreational purposes.

■■■ With the help of UNEP's Cleaner Production Programme, many industries are developing ways to reduce or eliminate the pollution they emit.

At present, too many large companies are engaged in bio-piracy, which involves taking plants and other life forms from developing countries and patenting the genetic material they extract. The Convention on Biological Diversity will oblige them to pay a fair price for any usage made of such material. If the money can be channeled to the local communities that are home to the plants and animals concerned, it would make a big difference, both in motivating people toward conservation and in providing them with the means to improve their living standards.

Unfortunately, the United States has not yet ratified the Biological Diversity Convention because of opposition from Congress. With time, Congress may be persuaded.

The Cartagena Protocol on Biosafety came into force in 2003, with more than 100 countries signing. Its objective is to ensure an adequate level of protection in the development, handling, transport, use, transfer, and release of living, modified organisms. This should be done in a manner that prevents or reduces risks to biological diversity and human health. The United States has not signed or ratified the Cartagena Protocol.

Worldwide, there is a huge number of people and organizations working to save the natural world. Vast data banks of environmental

---

Worldwide, there is a huge number of people and organizations working to save the natural world.

---

information have been created. Numerous conservation projects, both local and global, have been initiated. This international effort is taking place both in the field, among scientists and conservationists, and in meeting rooms, where politicians, business representatives, NGOs, and scientists discuss possible ways forward. Some suggest the

establishment of a new World Environment Organization to coordinate the action that is required. Perhaps a reformed United Nations can provide the impetus that is needed. The Rio de Janeiro Earth Summit of 1992 produced an astonishing degree of international agreement on the need for action to protect the environment. Although follow-up measures have been slow to come, no government has rejected the commitments made in Rio.

Programs such as the UNEP's Cleaner Production Programme, which promotes nonpolluting methods of manufacturing, and the Intergovernmental Forum on Forests are steps in the right direction. There is also increasing recognition that local communities and tribal groups are as important to the protection of biodiversity as scientists and ecologists. All is not yet lost, but it will take a big effort to save the world from the worst consequences of biodiversity loss.

MAIN ENVIRONMENTAL CONVENTIONS

Convention on Biological Diversity 1992 (effective 1993)

Ratified by more than 180 countries, the convention aims at the "conservation of biological diversity, the sustainable use of its components and the fair and equitable sharing of benefits arising out of the utilization of genetic resources."

Cartagena Protocol on Biosafety 2000 (effective 2003)

More than 100 countries have signed this protocol. Its objective is to ensure an adequate level of protection in the field of the safe transfer, handling, and use of living modified organisms resulting from modern biotechnology.

Convention on International Trade in Endangered Species of Wild Fauna and Flora (CITES) 1973 (effective 1975)

More than 160 countries are parties to this convention. Its goal is to ban trade in certain species of animal and plant, and to regulate trade in other threatened species. Wildlife trade is estimated at $20 billion a year, including illegal trade of some $5 billion.

Convention on Wetlands (Ramsar Convention) 1971 (effective 1975)

By December 2003, 138 contracting states had agreed to various protection measures covering 1,328 designated wetland sites, such as marshes, swamps, peatlands, lakes, and shallow marine waters. Worldwide, more than 276 million acres (112 million h) are covered, with Canada (13 million h), Russia (10.3 million h), Australia (7.3 million h), Brazil (6.4 million h) and Peru (6.7 million h) having the largest designated areas. Great Britain has the largest number of individually designated wetland sites (169). The Ramsar Convention is the only international convention that applies to a specific ecosystem. Wetlands provide an important breeding ground for many species of birds, fish, and plants.

Convention on Migratory Species (Bonn Convention) 1979 (effective 1983)

About 85 parties have signed this convention, which aims to protect 107 named species of bird and other threatened migratory animals.

Various other international conventions affect biodiversity, including those on climate change, and **desertification,** and the sea. Other international agreements protect land and marine areas, fisheries, or certain species of animals. The 1992 United Nations Conference on Environment and Development in Rio de Janeiro, Brazil, was the biggest-ever international conference on green issues. The 2000 International Union for Conservation of Nature's (IUCN) Second World Conservation Congress in Amman helped the process of consultation.

The World Heritage Convention gives protection to some of the world's most significant natural sites, and several hundred Biosphere Reserves have been designated by the United Nations Educational, Scientific and Cultural Organization (UNESCO). Regional agreements, such as the European Network of Biogenetic Reserves, adopted by the Council of Europe in 1976, add to the international measures designed to protect biodiversity. Many individual countries also have their own lists of protected sites. As of 2003, there are 440 biosphere reserves in 97 countries.

Some tomatoes have been genetically engineered to withstand frost.

KEY CONCEPTS

Genetic engineering Genetic engineering is the process by which the genetic makeup of a particular organism or species is manipulated in order to produce desirable traits or eliminate undesirable ones. Many benefits arise from genetic engineering. For example, plants can be engineered to contain nutrients otherwise unavailable in particular regions, and crops can be modified to be resistant to frost, drought, or certain pests. The full implications of genetically engineered plants have yet to be discovered.

Duties: Collecting, analyzing, and reporting data about the relationships among organisms in systems. Recommending to governments and nongovernmental organizations actions that should be taken to protect ecosystems.

Education: Bachelor of science degree in a related discipline, economics, or statistics

Interests: Working outdoors, mathematics, analyzing data, environmental health

Navigate to BLS Career Information
www.bls.gov/oco/ocos047.htm
for more information about ecologists and related careers.
Also click on **http://esa.sdsc.edu/ecologistsdo.htm** to see ecologist profiles.

Careers in Focus

Ecologists study the relationships among organisms and their environments. They examine the effects of influences such as population size, pollutants, rainfall, temperature, and altitude. Ecologists study whole ecosystems instead of focusing on a specific type of organism.

In addition to scientific knowledge, ecologists must have well-developed math and communications skills. Ecologists analyze scientific data and present their findings in reports, articles, and talks to the public. Most ecologists have an educational background in chemistry, environmental science, geology, biology, or climatology. Some have statistics and economics backgrounds. Most ecologists only perform studies outdoors for a few months each year. They spend most of their time at work in offices and laboratories analyzing the data they collect in the field. Most ecologists work for governments or for nongovernmental organizations, but some work for large corporations. Ecologists make recommendations that are used to plan and direct environmental policy.

Ecology is one of the fastest growing professions, owing to an increasing awareness of the importance of environmental health. As the world becomes more conscious of the extent and scope of the challenges facing the planet, the need for accurate ecological information increases. Often, ecologists are the first to document the changes in biodiversity in an area. Ecologists have studied and reported much of what we know about the environmental problems facing Earth.

Timeline of Events

1700

The Industrial Revolution begins in Great Britain.

1830

The human population is one billion.

1859

The rabbit is brought to Australia, soon overrunning the country and affecting ecosystems throughout the nation.

1890

The deadly infectious disease, rinderpest, diminishes the ungulate population of Africa.

1914

The last passenger pigeon known to exist on Earth dies at the Cincinnati Zoo.

1950

Global trade is estimated at $60 billion.

1971

The Convention on Wetlands occurs in Ramsar, Iran, with the mission of the conservation and wise use of all wetlands and their resources.

1973

The Convention on International Trade in Endangered Species of Wild Fauna and Flora occurs, with the goal to monitor trade in animal and plant species.

1979

The Convention on Migratory Species (Bonn Convention) is established to protect those species of wild animals that migrate across or outside national boundaries.

1990

The United Nations Statistical Division proposes a new accounting framework called the Integrated System of Environmental and Economic Accounts.

1990

Annual forest loss worldwide since 1990 is 23 million acres (9.4 million h). Most of this is natural forest in the tropics.

1992

The United Nations Conference on Environment and Development in Rio de Janeiro, Brazil occurs.

1993

The Convention on Biological Diversity becomes effective, with the goal of preserving biological diversity, and ensuring the sustainable use and equitable sharing of the benefits of biological diversity.

1994

The International Tropical Timber Agreement (ITTA) sets a goal of all tropical forest products coming from sustainably managed forests by the year 2000.

1997–98

The unusual weather events of El Niño–La Niña affect weather and climate worldwide.

1997

The United Nations designates this the Year of the Coral Reef.

1998

There is a significant coral bleaching event that ruined parts of the Indian Ocean, Southeast Asia, and the far western Pacific.

■■■ The white-tailed eagle, whose range covers most of Europe and Asia, has been extinct in Great Britain since the early 1900s. A reintroduction program has had minimal results.

1998
The United Nations designates this the Year of the Ocean.

2000
The loss of the world's reefs is assessed at 27 percent by the Global Coral Reef Monitoring Network.

2000
Twenty-four percent of mammal species and 12 percent of birds are considered globally threatened.

2000
The Food and Agriculture Organization of the United Nations estimates the world's forest at 10 billion acres (3.9 billion h).

2001
North American forest cover has expanded almost 10 million acres (4 million h) since 1991.

2001
The global fish catch of marine species is 91 million tons (8.3 million t). It has been at that level for more than a decade.

2002
Global trade is estimated at $7 trillion.

2003
The human population is more than six billion.

2003
The United States has the same area of forest as it did in 1920.

2005
Fears of human infection from pet birds causes the European Union to ban the import of all wild birds except poultry, after a parrot in Great Britain dies of the H5N1 strain of Asian bird flu.

2025 (projected)
The World Wildlife Fund anticipates there will be a loss of 20 percent of all species known to exist in 2003.

2103 (projected)
The human population will be more than 12 billion.

Concept Web

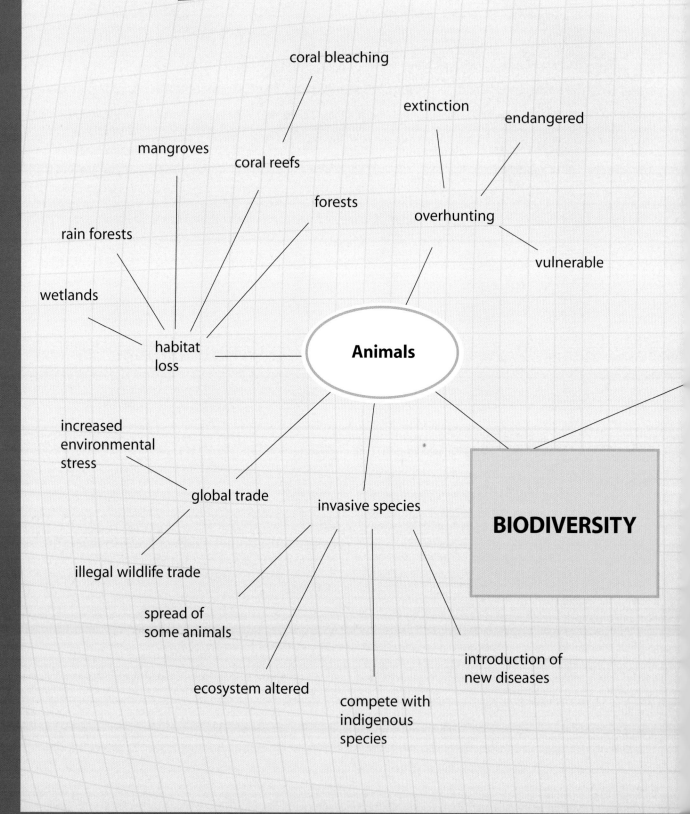

coral bleaching

extinction

endangered

mangroves

coral reefs

forests

overhunting

rain forests

vulnerable

wetlands

habitat loss

Animals

increased environmental stress

global trade

invasive species

BIODIVERSITY

illegal wildlife trade

spread of some animals

introduction of new diseases

ecosystem altered

compete with indigenous species

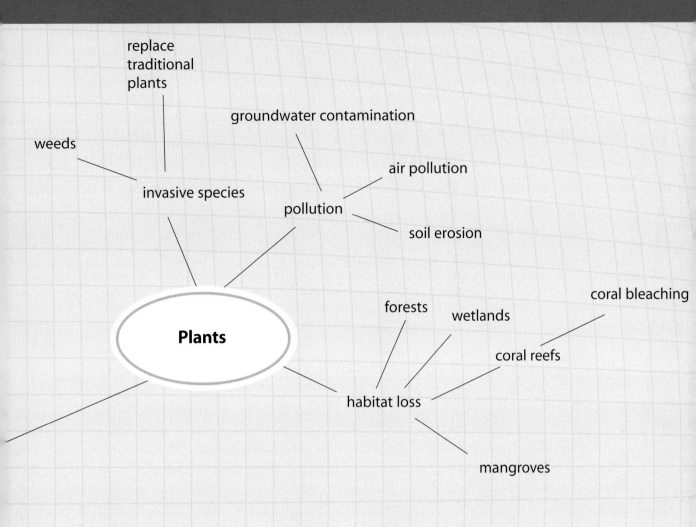

replace traditional plants

weeds

groundwater contamination

air pollution

invasive species

pollution

soil erosion

Plants

coral bleaching

forests

wetlands

coral reefs

habitat loss

mangroves

MAKE YOUR OWN CONCEPT WEB

A concept web is a useful summary tool. It can also be used to plan your research or help you write an essay or report. To make your own concept web, follow the steps below:

- You will need a large piece of unlined paper and a pencil.
- First, read through your source material, such as *Saving the Natural World* in the Understanding Global Issues series.
- Write the main idea, or concept, in large letters in the center of the page.
- On a sheet of lined paper, jot down all words, phrases, or lists that you know are connected with the concept. Try to do this from memory.
- Look at your list. Can you group your words and phrases in certain topics or themes? Connect the different topics with lines to the center, or to other "branches."
- Critique your concept web. Ask questions about the material on your concept web: Does it all make sense? Are all the links shown? Could there be other ways of looking at it? Is anything missing?
- What more do you need to find out? Develop questions for those areas you are still unsure about or where information is missing. Use these questions as a basis for further research.

Quiz

Multiple Choice

1. What are some disadvantages of global trade on the environment?
   a) It leads to the spread of disease.
   b) The link between the land and the community is broken.
   c) It means higher energy use, more roads, and more waste.
   d) all of the above

2. Food animals are:
   a) animals that eat other animals for food.
   b) animals, birds, or insects produced as food items for people to eat.
   c) pets that become food for other pets.
   d) all of the above

3. What is the primary issue of concern about genetic erosion?
   a) Food supplies do not increase.
   b) The world's basic food supply is vulnerable to new diseases, pests, or climate change.
   c) There is a depletion of species in the gene pool.
   d) It contributes to an unhealthy diet.

4. What has been the growth in the human population from 1830 to 2003?
   a) from 200,000 to 1 million
   b) from 5 million to 20 million
   c) from 5 billion to 15 billion
   d) from 1 billion to 6 billion

5. The World Wildlife Fund anticipates that if excessive hunting practices continue, by 2025 Earth could lose a large percentage of the species that exist today. This percentage is:
   a) 20 percent
   b) 44 percent
   c) 65 percent
   d) 80 percent

6. What percentage of the world's coral reefs had been lost by 2000?
   a) 60 percent
   b) 43 percent
   c) 37 percent
   d) 28 percent

7. How much is the trade in wildlife products worth every year?
   a) $10,000,000
   b) $20,000,000
   c) $500,000,000
   d)$1,000,000,000

Where Did It Happen?

1. The sea otter was hunted until it was believed to be extinct.
2. It has taken 25 years to destroy the native faunas in all lowland forests.
3. Mangroves are expanding after tin mines were abandoned.
4. Officials seized more than 800,000 animals or animal parts, many of them protected species.

True or False

1. Earth can sustain an increasing human population with no damage to its ecosystems.
2. The global fish catch of marine species has been at the same level for more than a decade.
3. Clear-cut logging is a cost-effective way to harvest forest resources.
4. Rich nations account for 20 percent of world population, but 85 percent of world pollution.

Answers on page 53

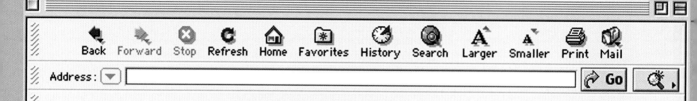

Internet Resources

The following websites provide information about biodiversity:

World Wildlife Fund
www.worldwildlife.org

The Energy Action website is a resource dedicated to energy conservation, environmental stewardship, and the promotion of positive action through better energy education. This website contains a section for students, which includes activities and a literature section.

United Nations Environment Programme—World Conservation Monitoring Centre
www.unep-wcmc.org

The World Conservation Monitoring Centre is the biodiversity assessment and policy arm of the United Nations Environment Programme. Its website provides information and statistics about world biodiversity, species, and habitats.

TRAFFIC International
www.traffic.org

Traffic International works to ensure that the wildlife trade does not result in the endangerment of any wild species or plant. This website provides detailed information about many aspects of the international wildlife trade.

Some websites stay current longer than others. To find other biodiversity websites, enter terms such as "biodiversity" and "conservation" into a search engine.

Further Reading

Brechin, Steven, Peter Wilshusen, and Crystal Fortwangler, editors. *Contested Nature: Promoting International Biodiversity and Social Justice in the Twenty-First Century.* New York: State University of New York Press, 2003.

Groombridge, Brian, and Martin Jenkins. *World Atlas of Biodiversity: Earth's Living Resources in the 21st Century.* Berkeley, California: University of California Press, 2002.

Lomborg, Bjorn. *The Skeptical Environmentalist: Measuring the Real State of the World.* New York: Cambridge University Press, 2001.

Lovelock, James. *Gaia: A New Look at Life on Earth.* Oxford: Oxford University Press, 2000.

Novacek, Michael, and the American Museum of Natural History. *The Biodiversity Crisis: Losing What Counts.* New York: New Press, 2001.

Rosenzweig, Michael. *Win-Win Ecology: How the Earth's Species Can Survive in the Midst of Human Enterprise.* Oxford, New York: Oxford University Press, 2003.

Wilson, Edward. *The Future of Life.* New York: Alfred A. Knopf, 2002.

Answers

Multiple Choice
1. d) 2. b) 3. b) 4. d) 5. a) 6. d) 7. b)

Where Did It Happen?
1. California 2. Sumatra, Indonesia 3. Phuket, Thailand 4. China

True or False
1. F 2. T 3. F 4. T

Glossary

ballast water: water held in tanks and cargo holds of ships to increase stability and maneuverability during transit

biomass: the total weight of all living organisms in a biological community

biosphere: the parts of Earth and its atmosphere in which living things are found

clear-cut logging: a section of forest where all trees have been cut down

desertification: deterioration of arid land into desert, caused by a change in climate or by overuse by people and animals

developing countries: countries that are undergoing the process of industrialization, sometimes collectively referred to as the "Third World"

ecosystems: systems formed by the interaction of plants and animals with the environment

ecotourism: tourism to places having unspoiled natural resources

evolution: the gradual development of a species or group of organisms

gross domestic product: the total monetary value of all goods and services produced in a country in one year, excluding payments on foreign investments

indigenous: native to a region

industrialized: having developed industry

Industrial Revolution: the change from an agricultural to an industrial society, which began in Great Britain in the mid-18th century and is continuing in some countries today

infrastructure: large-scale public systems, services, and facilities

nongovernmental organizations: nonprofit agencies that are independent from government

ozone: a form of oxygen in Earth's upper atmosphere that absorbs and prevents harmful ultraviolet rays from reaching Earth's surface

plankton: small or microscopic organisms that float or drift in great numbers in fresh or salt water and serve as food for fish and other large animals

species: a population of organisms that can produce fertile offspring

temperate: related to the geographic zones that lie between the tropics and the polar circles

tropical: related to the geographic zones that lie between the Tropic of Cancer and the Tropic of Capricorn

Index

Credits

All of the Internet URLs given in the book were valid at the time of publication. However, due to the dynamic nature of the Internet, some addresses may have changed, or sites may have ceased to exist since publication. While the author and publisher regret any inconvenience this may cause readers, no responsibility for any such changes can be accepted by either the author or the publisher.

Every reasonable effort has been made to trace ownership and to obtain permission to reprint copyright material. The publishers would be pleased to have any errors or omissions brought to their attention so that they may be corrected in subsequent printings.